For Raveen and Seven, the two I cherish the most.
—L.R.

Parent's Introduction

We Both Read is the first series of books designed to invite parents and children to share the reading of a story by taking turns reading aloud. This "shared reading" innovation, which was developed with reading education specialists, invites parents to read the more complex text and storyline on the left-hand pages. Then, children can be encouraged to read the right-hand pages, which feature less complex text and storyline, specifically written for the beginning reader.

Reading aloud is one of the most important activities parents can share with their child to assist them in their reading development. However, *We Both Read* goes beyond reading *to* a child and allows parents to share the reading *with* a child. *We Both Read* is so powerful and effective because it combines two key elements in learning: "modeling" (the parent reads) and "doing" (the child reads). The result is not only faster reading development for the child, but a much more enjoyable and enriching experience for both!

You may find it helpful to read the entire book aloud yourself the first time, then invite your child to participate in the second reading. In some books, a few more difficult words will first be introduced in the parent's text, distinguished with **bold lettering**. Pointing out, and even discussing, these words will help familiarize your child with them and help to build your child's vocabulary. Also, note that a "talking parent" icon ⬒ precedes the parent's text and a "talking child" icon ⬒ precedes the child's text.

We encourage you to share and interact with your child as you read the book together. If your child is having difficulty, you might want to mention a few things to help them. "Sounding out" is good, but it will not work with all words. Children can pick up clues about the words they are reading from the story, the context of the sentence, or even the pictures. Some stories have rhyming patterns that might help. It might also help them to touch the words with their finger as they read, to better connect the voice sound and the printed word.

Sharing the *We Both Read* books together will engage you and your child in an interactive adventure in reading! It is a fun and easy way to encourage and help your child to read—and a wonderful way to start them off on a lifetime of reading enjoyment!

We Both Read: Fox's Best Trick Ever

———————————————————

We Both Read® is a trademark of Treasure Bay, Inc.

Published by Treasure Bay, Inc.
40 Sir Francis Drake Boulevard
San Anselmo, CA 94960 USA

PRINTED IN SINGAPORE

Library of Congress Catalog Card Number: 2005911326

Hardcover ISBN-10: 1-891327-69-0
Hardcover ISBN-13: 978-1-891327-69-8
Paperback ISBN-10: 1-891327-70-4
Paperback ISBN-13: 978-1-891327-70-4

We Both Read® Books
Patent No. 5,957,693

Visit us online at:
www.webothread.com

WE BOTH READ®

Fox's
Best Trick Ever

By Dev Ross

Illustrated by Larry Reinhart

TREASURE BAY

One bright morning, Fox set out in search of breakfast. It wasn't long before he came upon **Bear,** who was eating **berries** he had picked from a bush that hung high over the river.

Fox wanted to eat **berries** too. Far too lazy to pick his own, he said, . . .

 "Hello, **Bear**. May I have your **berries**?

Bear said, "No." He did not want to give Fox his berries.

So Fox pointed at the river. "Never mind, Bear. I'll just eat *those* delicious looking berries down there."

Of course, *we* know the berries were really just a reflection in the water, but Bear didn't. So Bear jumped into the river after them!

Bear did not find any berries.

Cold and wet, Bear climbed back on shore to find that Fox had eaten every last one of his berries.

Fox was very clever. He had tricked Bear.

Bear was wet and
Bear was mad!

Fox was still hungry. So off he went in search of more food. It wasn't long before he came upon **Chipmunk**, who was busy collecting **acorns**.

Fox wanted to eat **acorns** too. Far too lazy to collect his own, he said, . . .

 "Hello, **Chipmunk**. May I have your **acorns**?"

Chipmunk said, "No." He did not want to give Fox his acorns.

So Fox pointed at a mountain. "Never mind, Chipmunk. I'll just eat that *big* acorn over there!"

Of course, we know the big acorn was really just a hill that looked like a big acorn, but Chipmunk didn't. So Chipmunk hurried toward the big acorn, leaving the real acorns behind.

Chipmunk did not find
a big acorn.

Chipmunk returned to see that Fox had eaten every last one of his acorns. Chipmunk had worked very hard to collect all of his acorns. Chipmunk did not like Fox taking things that didn't belong to him!

Chipmunk was sad
and he was mad!

Fox was still hungry, so off he went in search of more food. It wasn't long before Fox came upon **Eagle** and her nest full of eggs.

Fox liked eggs and so he said, . . .

 "Hello, **Eagle.** May I have your eggs?"

Eagle said, "No." She did not want to give Fox her eggs. So Fox pointed at a big **worm** that was crawling by. "Never mind, Eagle. I'll just eat that big juicy **worm** over there."

Of course, *we* know that Fox did not want to eat the **worm**. He wanted to eat Eagle's eggs. Guess what? Eagle knew that too!

Eagle said to Fox, . . .

"Please do. Eat the big **worm**. Eat it all up!"

Fox realized that he could not trick Eagle as easily as he had tricked Bear and Chipmunk. He would have to work harder.

So Fox *pretended* to eat the worm. While he was pretending, Fox said, . . .

"This big worm is good!
This big worm is great!"

Eagle had very good eyes. She saw that Fox was really pushing the big worm under a bush, so she said, "Look Fox! Look under the bush! There is *another* big worm for you to eat!"

Fox did not want to pretend to eat another big worm. He wanted to eat **eggs**! So he ran to Eagle's tree and shook it. He shook it so hard that Eagle's nest tumbled right over!

The **eggs** fell down
from the tree.

Fox opened his mouth to catch the eggs, but not one egg fell in. Instead Bear and Chipmunk **were** there to catch them and put them back in Eagle's nest. As they did, they scolded, . . .

"They are not your eggs!"

"They **were** not your berries!"

"They were not your acorns!"

Fox knew they were right and he knew what he had to do. He had to tell them that he was **sorry**.

But Fox did not say he was **sorry**. Fox ran away!

 Bear and Chipmunk just shook their heads sadly. Fox would never learn his lesson. There was nothing they could do.

But Eagle could do something. She flew after Fox then swooped down on top of him!

Fox went up in the air!

   Eagle carried Fox high into the sky. She carried him over snow capped mountains, above icy glaciers, and far out over the sea. She set Fox down on a tiny island and then flew off again.

   Eagle did not plan to leave Fox there long— just long enough to learn his lesson, but Fox did not know that.

Fox was sad and
he was sorry.

Fox knew he should have apologized to Bear, Chipmunk, and Eagle. He knew he should not take what wasn't his, but now it was too late.

Fox was so sad he began to sing: "A-om! A-om! I want to go home! A-he, A-he! I don't like the **sea**."

Walrus heard the song and popped his head out of the water to ask, . . .

"You do not like the **sea**?"

"No, I do not," sniffled Fox. "My home on land is better. The land has far more animals than the sea."

Walrus was sure this couldn't be true. He insisted the sea had far more animals in it than the land had on it. So Fox and **Walrus** quarreled back and forth.

"The land has more!"
said Fox.

"The sea has more!"
said **Walrus**.

To prove he was right, Walrus whistled and sea animals of all kinds popped their heads up out of the water. There were fish, seals, sea turtles, sharks, eels, starfish, and even a whale. There were enough sea animals to stretch all the way across the ocean and back again!

All of these animals gave Fox an idea.

Fox was going to play a trick. He was going to play his best trick ever!

Fox asked Walrus to line up all the animals in the sea so that he could count them. "Then we will know if there are more animals in the sea than there are animals on the land," he said.

Of course, we know that you could never count all the animals in the sea, but Walrus didn't.

Then Fox began to walk across the sea animals while counting, . . .

 "One, two, three, four, five, six, seven, eight, nine, ten . . ."

Fox walked and counted until Walrus could see him no longer. Then he walked and counted some more. Soon he had walked and counted all the way back to his home!

"So," asked little Crab, "are sea animals greater in number than land animals?" "I'm not sure," said Fox mischievously. "I'll go count the land animals and be right back." Off he ran.

Of course, *we* know that Fox never did come back, but Fox *did* learn a lesson!

Fox told Eagle that he was sorry. He told Chipmunk that he was sorry. He told Bear that he was sorry. That made everyone happy.

The End

Native American tales often use animal stories to teach lessons about life and help explain the world of nature. *"Fox's Best Trick Ever"* was adapted from a very old Inuit (pronounced In-yoo-it) tale that was passed down from adults to their children through the tradition of oral story telling.

The Inuit people are natives of Greenland, Northern Canada, Alaska, and the Sub-artic. While many Inuits can still build igloos, most of them now live in modern houses.

If you liked
Fox's Best Trick Ever, here are two other
We Both Read® Books you are sure to enjoy!

The young boy, Kibu, lives in Africa and is a member of the Masai tribe. When Kibu is told he is too small to go on the lion hunt, he decides to prove that he too can be a mighty lion hunter. With a basket of food from his mother he sets out into the African wilderness to find the biggest lion of all, Father Lion. With the help of some animal friends, Kibu hopes to outsmart Father Lion and return victorious.

To see all the We Both Read books that are available,
just go online to **www.webothread.com**

A wild ride of imagination awaits every reader of this
Level 1 story for beginning readers. Aunt Sue takes
her niece on a ride of adventure that brings them to
some places you can only find in a book! There's a
store with clothes that have cats and pans in the pock-
ets, a park with jogging frogs, and a zoo that is run by
the animals!